THE PRETEND LIFE

THE PRETEND LIFE
MICHELLE BROOKS

atmosphere press

Copyright © 2019 Michelle Brooks

Published by Atmosphere Press

Cover image by Don Brooks
Cover design by Nick Courtright

No part of this book may be reproduced except in brief quotations and in reviews without permission from the publisher.

10 9 8 7 6 5 4 3 2 1

The Pretend Life
2019, Michelle Brooks

atmospherepress.com

This book is dedicated to Emily Quane

TABLE OF CONTENTS

Leave It All on the Field	1
The Night Market of Ghosts	2
Ask About Our Daily Specials	3
Since God Could Not Be Everywhere	4
You're on Speaker	5
The Surprise Is the Price	6
Don't Be A Stranger	7
Your Time, Your Life	8
Kiss A Little Longer	9
It's Later Than You Think	10
Psychic Friends Network	11
Actual Persons, Living and Dead	12
Sealed for Your Protection	13
Don't Allow Yourself to Become A Victim	14
We Bring Good Things to Life	15
Refrigerate After Opening	16
No Reasonable Offer Refused	17
Fantasy World	18
Erase Your History	19
Everyone Loves to Pay Less	20
Don't Be A Stranger	21
Name Withheld Upon Request	22
You're Only Hurting Yourself	23
The Pretend Life	24
Entertainment for Men	25
We Deliver to the World	26
I Didn't Mean to Scare You	27
This Is Not A Metaphor	28
The Price of Admission	29
Safeway	30
Nothing to Declare	31
A Thousand Isn't Enough	32
All the Boys Want My Milkshake	33

No Parking Allowed Beyond This Point	34
Pick A Color	35
Notre Dame Is Burning	36
Where Dreams Come True	37
Flamethrower	38
Where the Negatives Are Buried	39
Take A Number	40
Do Not Adjust the Temperature	41
Watch What Develops	42
Camp Bowie at Night	43
These Things Happen	44
You Break It, You Buy It	45
Make A Wish	46
Sacrilege	47
Now Is Forever	48
Holograph Gallery	49
Exclusions May Apply	50

"It's a beautiful night. You can almost see the stars."
Repo Man

"Civilization is like a thin layer of ice upon a deep ocean of chaos and darkness." Werner Herzog

LEAVE IT ALL ON THE FIELD

A man less than a mile from my house
has shut down the highway. He's standing
on the bridge over which I drive almost
every day, and he's threatening to jump.
He won't despite people yelling, *Just
jump already* and *Kill yourself.* The police
close the road that leads to him, fearing
the shouts will push him over the edge.
This won't end until almost midnight.

I watch the Super Bowl, staring at the semi-
trucks and cars that have been diverted. They
creep past as I eat a bowl of French Onion dip.
The Eagles win, and fans trash the city, so great
their happiness. I'd like to say I don't understand
any of this, that I don't know what it's like to feel
too much or not enough. That I'd never stuffed pain
so deep that it both rots and explodes. I'd like to say
that things like this don't happen in my neighborhood.

THE NIGHT MARKET OF GHOSTS

The ground moves with snakes,
and the sky bleeds red streaks,
as if the night couldn't leave
without a fight, and all your dreams
are tragedies where no one dies,
but everyone suffers. In your past
life when you woke up hungover,
you'd think, *Anything is better than this*.

You were a confection, a little
dead around the eyes, the kind
of woman people describe as
pretty in a hard way. And you
refuse to go gently into that good
night. And let's face it. Not all
of them were good ones. You don't
care. There is nothing you can do
about it now. Gather the pieces
as best you can even if they cut you.

ASK ABOUT OUR DAILY SPECIALS

At the Molotov Cocktail, we serve
Irish Car Bombs all day, and our
napkins are rags soaked in kerosene.
Disasters unspool on our high-definition
televisions in surround sound – floods,
riots, mass shootings. Take your pick.
This Throwback Thursday, watch
Watts explode into flames at the bar.
Follow us on Facebook to discover
more vintage disasters and other special
offers. Leave a comment on our Instagram
if you have a suggestion for a disaster
you'd like to see. You can be anyone
here- lady killer, femme fatale, innocent
bystander. No one is a victim here. This
place only has so much room, and we
reserve the right to refuse service to anyone.

SINCE GOD COULD NOT BE EVERYWHERE

It looks cold out there, my mother said,
whenever skies went overcast,
forcing us into layers and jackets,
no matter the temperature. I loved
this sweet maternal tick in a woman
whose own life had offered little
in the way of benign comforts. It's another
Mother's Day, and she's still gone. I guess
that's not going to change. When she felt
stressed, my mother made lists, *Things To Do
Today* and *From The Desk Of* scraps littered
the house, some items never crossed.
I think of my own lists, the ones written
between the lines. And when the sky clouds
and it's warm, I find myself chilled, as if
the way it looked were enough to make it true.

YOU'RE ON SPEAKER

The story I can tell isn't dramatic. I'm
sure you can relate. It's about horrible
things that happened to me, by me. It's
about secrets, open and otherwise, all
the ones I clutched so hard that my nails
bit into my skin. I carried them like my
life depended on it, and I forgot why,
and I forgot what it was to be free of them.
They rattled inside me, and nothing bad
happened, did it? I swallowed the evidence,
and the evidence swallowed me. The world is
lost, and I don't even know where to begin to look.

THE SURPRISE IS THE PRICE

And when I see you and the person
with me says, *Who's that?* I'll say,
*Nobody. Just someone I thought
I knew.* I will hide the trace of you in my
face, the past like a shard, making every
movement a limp. Even so, no one
will notice. You taught me so many
ways to hide. Even so, don't flatter
yourself. I have no secrets. I am the rumor
you don't believe, the story that can't be true.

THE LUMINOUS MYSTERIES

For the better part of an hour, I sit
in an examination room, my nose
dripping onto the butcher paper,
having feigned interest in the fake
breast handed to me by a doctor
at this urgent care. I had only hoped
for a quick shot of antibiotics to make
me well once more. After the door
shuts, I drape my red coat over my legs,
the coat I bought at a thrift store in Grosse
Pointe, only a few miles from this decimated
city, Detroit, I loved upon first sight.
The doctor instructed me to practice
on this model until he returned with a script.
He takes my word for my condition, and grabs
the breast from my hand, telling me a girl
can never be too careful, and self-exams
are the first line of defense. I nod, trying
to finish the decade of the rosary I started.
Don't ask me how I ended up here.
I've never been good at directions.

DON'T BE A STRANGER

There is nothing to see here,
just memories that aren't yours,
and days you will never get back,
and the sense you will never escape
yourself, and I remember a girl
in my old neighborhood who shared
my name. The adults said she was
touched, a little slow. That summer,
the Bicentennial, everyone adorned
themselves with flags. Bruce Jenner
won the Decathlon, and women talked
in hushed tones about rumors of affairs,
of husbands who beat their wives.
The world was still a mystery, as was
the day the father of the sweet little
girl who shared my name came home
from repairing air-conditioning units
and shot her and her mother before
killing himself. The house where I grew
up remains the same, iron bars covering
the windows, still protecting everyone
in the house from everything but themselves.

YOUR TIME, YOUR LIFE

You feel like you've seen this movie
already. There's a man who no one
realizes is bad. Or maybe someone
does, but no one listens to the warning.
It's almost too late for the woman,
his girlfriend, fiancé, wife. She ignores
all the signs until she can't. He's not
who he pretends to be. His motives
don't really matter. They never do.

There are no monsters here, just predators
and victims. There's a lot of running,
driving, glances meant to signal danger.
You are too tired to turn the channel.
The woman in these movies always
lances back. The man is forward motion
until he returns to the scene of the crime.
That's his mistake. As for you, who knows?
No good can come from such reflection!
You already know how this one ends.

KISS A LITTLE LONGER

If you were mine, I'd wear
lingerie every night, and I'd
always know what you wanted
for lunch, and I'd give you
truth serum for your birthday,
and I would keep all my secrets
in a locked miniature hope chest
I received as a free gift with purchase
at Dillards when I turned eighteen.
And you? Don't worry your pretty little
head. You wouldn't realize what hit you.

IT'S LATER THAN YOU THINK

There is the reflection of a rainbow
in the Rent to Own window, and puddles
have formed in the holes dotting the parking
lot, the water streaked with rainbows made
of gasoline, and I try to remember what I need
for tomorrow's work party as I roam the Dollar
General. I grab a bag of pretzels and think,
This is my dinner and all the while, other lives
play out around me. A teenager tells her friend,
*I can't believe Halloween is tomorrow, and I don't
know what I'm going to be. I wasn't anything last
year.* A man asks his wife, *Do you think the rain
has stopped?* She doesn't look at him, only
says, *I sure fucking hope so. It's depressing.*

After loading my basket with paper plates
adorned with skulls and witches, I get in line,
looking down while the young couple in front of me
buys a pregnancy test and a bag of Cheetos,
the woman counting out change from a tiny
purse embossed with stars. The cashier, a middle-aged
woman with *Bitch* tattooed on her neck asks me
if I found what I needed. I nod and say yes, thinking
does anyone? The cashier leans close, warns me
that a man has been following me around the aisles
and asks if I want security to walk me out. I thank her,
saying I'll make a run for it, as I gather up my bags.
The rain has started again. I glance back, relieved
no one is following me, noticing the sign festooned
over the door, *Spooky Savings Inside*, as if I wouldn't know.

PSYCHIC FRIENDS NETWORK

Do you want to know the future?
There is none. The future is now.
You are the future. Scratch that.
Children are the future. The future
is what you make it. Okay, I get it.
Let's start over. I know what you want.
You will meet a mysterious stranger.
You have an old soul. That person you're
worried about? All will be well. Am
I getting warmer? My godmother met
a man through the personal ads. He
murdered her. You know those stories
because the past never ever goes away.
The future doesn't matter. Try not
to be afraid. I'm here in the dark with you.

ACTUAL PERSONS, LIVING OR DEAD

Let's turn on the lights.
Ghosts drift toward shadows.
Use the sin of omission as if
it were a life raft, and you can't
swim. I can swim, of course.
As a child I swam in tanks,
throwing rocks before getting
into the water to scatter the snakes
while my mother doled out advice:
If you fall out of a boat, float.
You can float forever. I never learned
how to float, always defaulting to treading
water. You can do that for a long time.

SEALED FOR YOUR PROTECTION

If I were a locksmith, I'd call
my company Open Sesame
and I'd list my services in free
circulars, and I'd be able to open
anything except myself and this
would be the price I paid for my
gifts. While you breathe a sigh
of relief as you walk into your
life, I would wait for someone
to break my windows, as if I
were the one thing that mattered,
struggling to hide the inevitable
surprise finding nothing inside.

DON'T ALLOW YOURSELF TO BECOME A VICTIM

The noise, constant, felt like a blanket
of quiet, and intrusions of silence opened
like a cut, unexpected, awful, a gaping
wound that needed to be covered lest it
allow entry into the blood. Let's face it.
I am broken, and nothing should touch me.
I am alone, and the night surrounds me. I hear
snippets of songs blaring from cars, *You
don't know what it's like to be me*. Girls
huddle together, their laughter punctuated
by cigarettes, high heels, lipstick, and hope.
The dark pulses with need, all lit by the stunning,
lonesome artificial lights that promise what it
can and cannot give, and nothing else matters,
and nobody blinks in the endless darkness.

WE BRING GOOD THINGS TO LIFE

You run through my memory
like electricity,
unseen and omnipresent,
benign for the most part.

I once shocked myself on a cheap Wal-Mart
lamp, my hands clenched around the black stand,
unable to let go until someone knocked it out
of my grasp. I couldn't help but think, *What if
this had happened when I was alone?* I threw
away the lamp and never replaced it, content
with the glow from outside. Who needs to see
everything clearly? I knew the electricity had
forced my muscles to tense, my grip tightening
around that which would do me harm. It's natural.
I am not exempt. Please try not to remind me.

REFRIGERATE AFTER OPENING

The day turns into a smudge,
and I wonder where the time
goes, the darkness visible now.
It all happened without warning.
When I get used to one thing, it
becomes another, and I am
powerless to turn back. Nights,
I flip between channels. The day
of salvation is at hand, and I can
prepare with Time of Trouble food
pantry bundle (*Imagine the world is
dying and you're having the breakfast
of kings!*). On another channel, I can
buy a tomato shark and get another
for free, plus shipping and handling.

I fall asleep in front of this cacophony
of possibility, dreaming of the time
I was cast as the Ghost of Christmas Past,
a part I practiced in a church basement
before the performance was cancelled.
I never got to present the shadows of things
that have been and nobody wore the chains
they forged in life that December. Now
I sleep in a chain with a bullet dangling
from it, lulled by the shadows of what
will never be, the disembodied voices
a lullaby, my bullet a charm to ward
off the ghosts of this season, any season.

NO REASONABLE OFFER REFUSED

I survey the discount hearts, already
dented from the hands of customers
who didn't choose them, the flowers
adorned with signs announcing *For
Someone Special* stand at attention,
the bouquets wilting like understudies
whose big break isn't going to happen.
I want to tell them, *Don't give up. I see
how beautiful you are!* I rummage
through the bins, pick up a box of candy
with *Be Mine* in wedding cake font scrawled
across the front and put it in my basket,
avoiding the conversation hearts, ones
that say things like, *U R Great.* There's only
so much I can take, and after all, I know better.

FANTASY WORLD

Every night here is the same.
At first you don't notice. You
can't. Don't worry. It's all designed
to excite. You can't see any flaws
in the dim lights, the music covers
the lack of conversation. And still.
It gets predictable. But no matter how
bored you become, you can't stay away
for too long. Just try. You miss the trace
of the crushed flowers, the girls whose
eyes get a little deader each day. Once
you know what's in the recipe, can you
still order it? Or do you continue because
you've become the excuse the girls
use for staying, *It beats working
for nothing*. You're work, you see --
the kind a girl takes home with her even
though she promised herself she wouldn't.

ERASE YOUR HISTORY

These are the pictures that aren't
on my computer, the family album
my mother kept, the snapshots of parties,
vacations, life. In this world, I wear
a blue bikini, my six-year old self
posing on the porch with a tiny flag,
the Bicentennial year in full swing.

That was the year the teenage son
of Bobby and Hazel, my parents' friends,
died. I think of Johnny Mac, buried near
his grandparents, while the sky exploded
into color. He'd be fifty now. In this place
he's still a shy boy, captured on the motorcycle
that he rode into the unfathomable hereafter.

All the adults I remember at his graveside
have joined him. I miss them all, miss those
endless nights of adults drinking and smoking
inside the house. Before I entered this new
world, the one where I am haunted by a history
no one knows. I put the album into the closet,
promising myself I will place the pictures
into a newer version, one that promises to preserve
and protect your images, not like the old type
of album that damages everything you put in it.

EVERYONE LOVES TO PAY LESS!

Everything is discounted now,
and I browse the almost empty
shelves, as if some treasure might
present itself. I pick up a generic
black high heel and am filled
with grief, as if someone I knew
died instead of an old store in a strip
mall, one I thought would be open
forever if I cared to pay it a visit.
I wonder what will happen to the shoes
that don't sell, if someone will wear
them as she wonders where to go
for lunch or if it's time to leave
for work, while the heartbreaking world
dies and resurrects around her feet.

NAME WITHHELD UPON REQUEST

The moon, a fingernail of light tonight,
appears, and I return home late. I don't
have anywhere else to be, and you don't
have anywhere else to go. I unpack groceries,
stuffing the plastic bag into a drawer
with other plastic bags. *We should throw
these out,* I say. *We're never going to use
them.* You agree, but your heart isn't in it.
I should know. You like to keep everything.

YOU'RE ONLY HURTING YOURSELF

I pretend not to see you – reasons
include but are not limited to not
wearing any make-up, unflattering
work-out pants, the circles beneath my
eyes. I hide behind a display of cereal,
pretending to read the nutritional information
on a box of Lucky Charms, holding my
breath until I see you creep toward self-
check-out. What can I say? We left each
other worse than before, so very predictable.
I am your broken window.
And you can never fix me.

THE PRETEND LIFE

If I lived in the Oak Shadows
trailer park, I'd want my trailer
to be the color of a 7Up bottle,
I'd want to be beautiful and young.
I'd want to be beloved by someone who
couldn't live without me. I'd be
tragic, a little dead around the eyes.
I'd live in the space before everything
begins. I'd be no one you know,
a shadow on the concrete, a flash
of color you might see as you drove
by me on your way to somewhere else.

ENTERTAINMENT FOR MEN

The tanning beds at Foxy Jeans were housed
in the back room, side by side, twin coffins
containing the sun. For twenty-five dollars a month,
you could tan as often as you wanted. Adventurous
types availed themselves of the complimentary *Playboy*
stickers provided by management. They placed
the decals on their naked bodies, a white mark
preserved against their darkening skin. Most never
lined up the stickers the same way twice, the icon
mutating until it looked as if the bunnies had been
born after a nuclear accident, the product of poisoned
land. I could never bring myself to seal my body
into one of the beds, trapped in the artificial brightness,
no matter how many women flashed me a hip, a butt cheek,
or cleavage adorned with their deformed bunnies, proud
of what they'd done, assuring me it was worth the trouble.

WE DELIVER TO THE WORLD

It's nearing the shortest day
of the year, the light the color
of amber, and my life feels like
an adult dragging me along as I
struggle to keep up, worse for wear.
Images flicker around me, promising
things will be different this time.
I hesitate before the window in this
cold ICU room, stare at the flower
shop across the street and notice
clouds forming in the distance. A man
down the hall screams, *Is it my time?
Are you going to take me now, Jesus?*
while Tom Cruise saves the world
on the small screen, noise intended
to mask the beeping of machines.
The flower shop sign says, We Deliver
to the World! which I assume contains
this room where I wait for nothing
good to happen. That's all left to do.

I DIDN'T MEAN TO SCARE YOU

A girl crawls out of the dumpster
at the Shell where I am getting gas
early Sunday morning, the heat already
like a blanket. In the bleached
denim light, I gather empty water
bottles and fast food wrappers to toss
while the girl motions to someone
who crawls out of the dumpster which
appears to contain multitudes. I curse
myself for letting the tank get to almost
empty while the numbers rise. My Russian
nesting dolls from the dumpster walk
into an alley, gone from my sight. Did
they find what they were looking for?
Does anyone? All I know is that gas prices
are rising again, making me wonder why
it costs so much to get anywhere at all.

THIS IS NOT A METAPHOR

The *Twilight Zone* theme song played
from the phone I dropped in the grave
yard the day before, and I limped in the early
morning fog as it called to me, having jumped
the fence with two broken toes to take
pictures of the long-buried dead, most
of them interred long before I was born.
Do they watch as I crawl around their tomb
stones, looking for a device they couldn't
have imagined? I can talk to anyone, anywhere.
I always know the weather. But the only words
that matter here are the ones carved in stone,
and nobody cares about   tomorrow.

THE PRICE OF ADMISSION

There is something I don't want
to tell you, and I will pretend
that I am fine, so that you don't
make it worse. And don't kid yourself.
You can always make it worse.
Even if you only hurt me on the way
to better, nothing is certain, and I'd
rather slit my own throat than take
a risk. You see, I'm a romantic,
and I prefer to pay for everything.

SAFEWAY

Somewhere I am not, beautiful women
and mysterious men are drinking at bars
laced with possibility, serving top-shelf
concoctions. The years' relentless march
doesn't take me to these places. Instead, I
am alone in a grocery store, eyeing produce.
I don't care what I get. I can't afford
to be picky when all the perishables are
going bad with each passing second.

NOTHING TO DECLARE

You don't have to do anything
except keep your mouth shut. Try
to forget. Your secret requires nothing
of you. You do not feed it or water it,
or buy it gifts and find a place to store
it. Bury it within yourself with no marker
to let people know it's there. And it isn't.
Anyone can see your hands are empty.
What no one notices is that your hands
tremble slightly. It's nothing really.
Your life is a door you keep closing, ever
so quietly no one notices you're gone.

A THOUSAND ISN'T ENOUGH

It's that kind of the night, after
a day where you've consumed almost
nothing, gliding through the work day
hours with purpose. You didn't slow
down. And now you are outside
in the spring air and summer presses
on you like a rumor and you can be
anyone. You have overridden the controls,
bribed the guard in your head to take
a break. You are free to tumble into oblivion.
You don't think about the morning. You
don't think. You want the mysteries
of the darkness. What you don't know
is obvious to anybody who bothered
to look. You have already become one.

ALL THE BOYS WANT MY MILKSHAKE

I saw through a glass darkly, and in truth,
many glasses full of potions that burned
like hellfire. I developed nervous tics,
my right eye twitching, even as I played
Truth or Dare. I didn't have any use for truth
so I took the dare and managed a partial
striptease to LL Cool J's "Don't Call It
A Comeback." Don't worry. I'm not coming
back. Hollowed out, dead around the eyes, my
voice mail remains full. If you happen to call
me, you won't be able to leave anything.

NO PARKING ALLOWED BEYOND THIS POINT

A girl in fishnets walks down the street
staring at her phone before sitting
on the curb, head in her hands. I'm stopped
at a red light, cursing another Monday
morning. I drive away before the girl
stands up, and I wonder what sorrows have visited
her from across the transom, what sadness lives
in the invisible waves that have travelled
through her phone. I park and walk to my
office and a man yells out of his truck window,
Do you want to party? I do not. I smile, look
down and see a rip in my tights. It's too early
for this shit, and it's too late to change.
The man persists until I look at him, shake
my head as I slide my keys between my fingers
that I have somewhere else I have to be.

PICK A COLOR

The man tells me he's from Chicago
where the women are really picky.
He likes that they know what they want.
I sit in the chair watching as he files
my nails. I'm not picky and what I want
is a secret I hide from myself. *Just black?*
he asks. *No flower design? I do beautiful
flowers.* He's full of suggestions, none
of which I take. I praise his work, and he
smiles like I'm boring him. I've been here
many times, this nail salon in Detroit,
and we all know what we don't want.
The next time I see him, he's painting
someone else's nails, his torso slumped over,
as if defeated by this piece of the Midwest
where on most days, the sky is devoid
of any color except concrete gray.

NOTRE DAME IS BURNING

You left months ago, and I became
a ghost, haunting my own life for clues.
Nothing changes until it does. We are
left with ashes – my heart burns
and I don't know if I will ever not feel it.
The firefighters in Paris saved some
of the statues, and many were moved
for restoration, removed on wires, the glorious
saints flying through the air to another destination.

Without you, my life is a salvage yard.
I wander through shadows
the ones that flicker on television,
watching the all-consuming fire. When
they announce that they have saved
the crown of thorns, I think, *That sounds right.*

WHERE DREAMS COME TRUE

The bathroom attendant asks me when
my shift begins. In my silver dress, I look
like a shake dancer. Soon, I tell her, giving
her a dollar for the peppermint she offers me.
I look for my friends, the sounds of the casino,
of luck and loss, surround me. I spot a dwarf
wearing a beret adorned with glitter riding
a scooter. He wheels toward me and yells,
"What are you looking at?" I tell him I'm
waiting for my shift to start, and he softens.
"First day?" he asks. I nod. "Shake it like you
mean it," he says, rolling away to put quarters
in the Count Chocula slot machine. I find my
friends at the bar ordering expensive cocktails
that appear as if they are on fire, smoke from dry
ice enveloping them until you're left with vodka
and fruit juice. I take a sip, thinking about how
I could get the same thing for half the price down
the street but I'm not paying for the drink. You
never pay for just the drink. You pay for the show.

FLAMETHROWER

If I were a weapon, I'd be a Molotov
Cocktail, poised in the hand of a revolutionary.
Cheap and easy to make, I'd explode once,
sacrificing the container to set the known
world ablaze. And if I were a potion,
I'd be truth serum, and you'd tell me secrets
that you had concealed even from yourself.
I'd infect your blood with the promise
of liberation. And if I were a plant, I'd be
Poison Hemlock streaked with purple
and red. Who knows? Maybe you'd pick
me, mistaking me for something harmless.

WHERE THE NEGATIVES ARE BURIED

The city recedes until even
this receding leaves me.
I know from that one story
that no one can reside in paradise
forever. Paradise only reveals
itself as such in the rearview
mirror. This space between what
was and what is, this purgatory,
I do not leave it. I cannot let
the dead bury the dead. I become
the negative of a picture, one
I never allow myself to develop.

TAKE A NUMBER

It's September, and I'm thinking
about every office job I've ever
held, about the feeling of three
o'clock on any random Wednesday
afternoon, the feeling of my life
leeching away with the light. I'm
thinking of nights when the choice
is between frozen pizza and leftovers,
of the multi-packs of chips in which
only the bland ones remain, of waiting
at the DMV, of football games blaring
in the background on any given Sunday,
of bills to pay and errands to run. When I
die, I will miss it all. It's September.

DO NOT ADJUST THE TEMPERATURE

You don't love me and that's
okay. Any trace of emotion is like
breakthrough bleeding – nothing
to worry about. You don't know me.

And I blame you, just like I said
I wouldn't. I'm sorry, just like I
knew I would be. Day follows
night. The circle remains unbroken.
It never occurred to me that a broken
heart remains whole enough to break,
that just because you strike through
a word doesn't mean it isn't still there.

WATCH WHAT DEVELOPS

I have never been to Coney Island
yet the Ferris wheel in sepia-drenched
pictures, the greenish tint of old Polaroids,
the relics rendered in black and white
fill me with a past I will never know.
And yet it is mine, a ghost that speaks
my name as if I'd been there, haunted
by rides I never took, the fun I never had.

CAMP BOWIE AT NIGHT

Working girls huddle in front
of hotels, their burning cigarettes
punctuating the night like fireflies,
exclamation points that will be
discarded without ceremony. Sinbad's,
"The Classiest Strip Club with the Most
Beautiful Girls," advertises an all-you-can-
eat buffet. It used to be a Red Lobster.
My parents took my sister and me there
to celebrate birthdays. I longed for a hot-
pink sequined tube top, sandals that turned
into roller skates when you pushed a button
on the cork-lined heel, a black silk robe to wear
while listening to Grover Washington Jr's
Winelight and drinking champagne. It's all
different now. And yet the desire only morphs,
never satiated. I stop at Walgreens, hear glass
shatter somewhere in the night. When I return
to my car, I see pieces of a pipe strewn
about like confetti. It only held smoke,
so half-full or half-empty doesn't apply.

THESE THINGS HAPPEN

After I find out, I think of how
Crayola retired Dandelion, a color
I almost never used as a child. Still,
I miss it before it's gone, like every
day of my life. He told me it would
never happen again, and my best friend
said, *She could have been anyone.*
And I think that sounds wonderful,
like walking out of my life, closing
the door one last time before disappearing.
It beats my usual trick, the one where I lie
in a box and let someone cut me in half.
Even an illusion can wear on the soul.
The real trick is simple – never look back.

YOU BREAK IT, YOU BUY IT

My haunted house looks
like a shadow box filled
with silences that no one
can break, ghosts only I see.

When something breaks
something I can't live
without, I live. I don't
wonder if it's fragile because
it's delicate and rare
or it's poorly made. Make
no mistake. Nothing is cheap.

MAKE A WISH

You are not dead yet, or if you
are no one has told you. In Best
Buy, you see a huge poster that says
Make A Wish and a bald girl wheels
around the store picking out movies. A limo
waits outside for her to whisk her away
to lunch. No Disneyland in Detroit for
sick children and the efforts to make
her small desires come true, if only for a few hours,
breaks you as you buy printer paper.
You wonder what her name is until someone
announces it over the PA, the same as yours,
a common name, unexceptional except for this
strange coincidence. You drift through the aisles
of devices promising distraction, salvation only
implied, never guaranteed. What is certain is that
you will walk out the doors with less money,
less time, a subtle diminishment. You came
into the world with nothing so you're used to it.
It begs the question, *Why does it feel so awful?*

SACRILEGE

I live in dark circles under
my eyes, as if the night I carry
leaks through my skin. Every
morning tells my secrets,
a partially erased chalkboard
where I sought to obliterate
the past, now reduced to this
lump in my throat. I could
hunt my ancestors like Easter
eggs if I wanted, but it is enough
to carry the dead, their violent
love, their casual murderous
rages, against what I can only
guess. After all, this is the first
day of the rest of my life. Yet
despair sets in like dye, and I
dress as if I have somewhere
to go, anywhere but here.
The joke is on me. I meet
myself at every fire escape,
but there is no fire, just matchbooks
from places that no longer exist.

NOW IS FOREVER

And it is written:
You belong to no one.
Yet the dead own me.
What am I to make
of this strange paradox?
I see faces in the bathroom
mirror. I think they miss
this house where I now
live. Perhaps they are
trapped? Who, after all,
can tell the difference
between longing and duty?
But when I look again, they
disappear as if they were
never there at all. And I
thought that was my story.

HOLOGRAPH GALLERY

In the eighties, my childhood, people
liked to see through things, to watch
the inner workings. It didn't matter
what – clocks, pianos, you name it.
There is nothing here to see, no bolts,
no gears to watch. It is because I'm too
deep to penetrate? Or because there are
none? Do you believe in ghosts? You
should. I don't mean the kind that pay you
the occasional visit. I mean the ones that are
always with you, the ones that cling. I would
say *like death*, but that should be obvious.
Confused? You should be. Just try to leave.

EXCLUSIONS MAY APPLY

There's something, he said, *about the way she loves me then doesn't. She's a cold, beautiful city that I've only seen on posters.* I laughed and said, *And I thought I was the poet.* He smiled, the kind of smile a doctor offers you before a terminal diagnosis. *You've never been in love with someone who doesn't love you.* I shake my head, try to sympathize. But nothing is ever enough, and we both agree, that's the problem. *We're too old for this shit,* he adds, wondering if he should call her. I tell him that nobody calls anyone these days. It's all text. *Is it late enough for a drink?* he asks. I say what I always do, *Where's the harm?* It's always late enough. Maybe it just seems like it should be late enough somewhere, anywhere.

ACKNOWLEDGMENTS

I'd like to thank my family and friends, living and dead, without whom this book would not exist. I offer my deepest gratitude to Beth Brooks, Angela Bills, Emily Quane, Hank Ballenger, Brad Foster, Don and Margie Brooks, Marci Anderson, Trent Vanegas, Black Cat Press, Linda and Jim Mueller, Laura and Pinkney Benedict, Shawn Behlen, Sharon Serra, Robin Konarz, my Detroit friends (Stacey, Jodi, Mark, Tim), Ken Mandel, Barb, Vickie, Linda, Jamie, Donna Ballenger, Peter and Connie, Dominic Baffo, Deacon John at St. Sylvester's, Daniel Mueller, and all those people who have supported and loved me, too numerous to mention. Thanks to all the journals that published these poems and to Nick Courtright and Caitlin Cowan at Atmosphere Press. And thanks to Saint Jude, who never fails.

Leave It All on the Field – *Free State*
The Night Market of Ghosts – *The Lake*
Ask About Our Daily Specials – *Contemporary Expressions*
Since God Could Not Be Everywhere – *Manzano Literary Review*
The Luminous Mysteries – *Flying Island*
Your Time, Your Life – *Cholla Needles*
Kiss A Little Longer – *Red Weather*
It's Later Than You Think – *Sierra Nevada Review*
Actual Persons, Living and Dead – *Black Fox Literary Review*
Sealed for Your Protection – *Worcester Review*
Don't Allow Yourself to Become A Victim – *Anapest Paragon Press*
We Bring Good Things to Life – *Red Weather*

Refrigerate After Opening – *Rise Up Review*
No Reasonable Offer Refused – *Hamilton Stone Review*
Fantasy World – *Poetry Circle*
Erase Your History – *Cape Rock Review*
Name Withheld Upon Request – *Deluge Literary Review*

You're Only Hurting Yourself – *Constellations*
The Pretend Life – *Sky Island Review*
Entertainment for Men – *Typishly*
We Deliver to the World – *Consumnes River Review*
I Didn't Mean to Scare You – *Anapest Paragon Press*
Nothing to Declare – *Negative Capability Press*
A Thousand Isn't Enough – *Cholla Needles*
All the Boys Want My Milkshake – *Heartland Review*
No Parking Allowed Beyond This Point – *Sand Hills Literary Journal*
Where Dreams Come True – *The Southern Collective*
Flamethrower – *Apeiron Review*
Take A Number – *Broadkill Press*
Do Not Adjust the Temperature – *New Gaia Press*
Watch What Develops -- *Litbreak*
Nothing to Declare – *The Southern Collective*
Exclusions May Apply – *Dime Show Review*
Camp Bowie at Night – *Evening Street Press*
These Things Happen – *New Plains Review*
You Break It, You Buy It – *Cholla Needles*
Holograph Gallery – *The Helix*
Don't Be A Stranger – *Broadkill Press*

ABOUT ATMOSPHERE PRESS

Atmosphere Press is an independent, full-service publisher for excellent books in all genres and for all audiences. Learn more about what we do at atmospherepress.com.

We encourage you to check out some of Atmosphere's latest poetry releases, which are available at Amazon.com and via order from your local bookstore:

Minnesota and Other Poems, by Daniel N. Nelson

Interviews from the Last Days, by Christina Loraine

the oneness of Reality, by Brock Mehler

Drop Dead Red, by Elizabeth Carmer

Aging Without Grace, by Sandra Fox Murphy

No Home Like a Raft, by Martin Jon Porter

Mere Being, by Barry D. Amis

They are Almost Invisible, by Elizabeth Carmer

Auroras over Acadia, by Paul Liebow

Transcendence, by Vincent Bahar Towliat

Adrift, by Kristy Peloquin

Time Do Not Stop, by William Guest

Ghost Sentence, by Mary Flanagan

What Outlives Us, by Larry Levy

What I Cannot Abandon, by William Guest

All the Dead Are Holy, poetry by Larry Levy

ABOUT THE AUTHOR

Michelle Brooks grew up in Mineral Wells, Texas, a small town on the edge of west Texas. Her work has appeared in *Hayden's Ferry Review, Gargoyle, Threepenny Review, Iowa Review, Alaska Quarterly Review, Hotel Amerika, and elsewhere.* She has published a collection of poetry, *Make Yourself Small*, (Backwaters Press), and a novella, *Dead Girl, Live Boy*, (Storylandia Press). Her photographs have appeared in *Shadows and Light, Alchemy, Literary Heist,* and elsewhere. Upon graduating from the University of North Texas, she moved to Detroit, Michigan, her favorite city.

CPSIA information can be obtained
at www.ICGtesting.com
Printed in the USA
LVHW090856211119
637710LV00040B/436/P